I Call
My Grandmother
Nonna

A Collection of Stories

by
Bruna Di Giuseppe-Bertoni

ISBN: 978-0-9951765-0-8

This is the original print edition of *I Call My Grandmother Nonna.*

To my grandchildren:
Franca, Julia, Jessica, Arturo, Maia, and Daphne;
and to my great-grandchild, Adrian

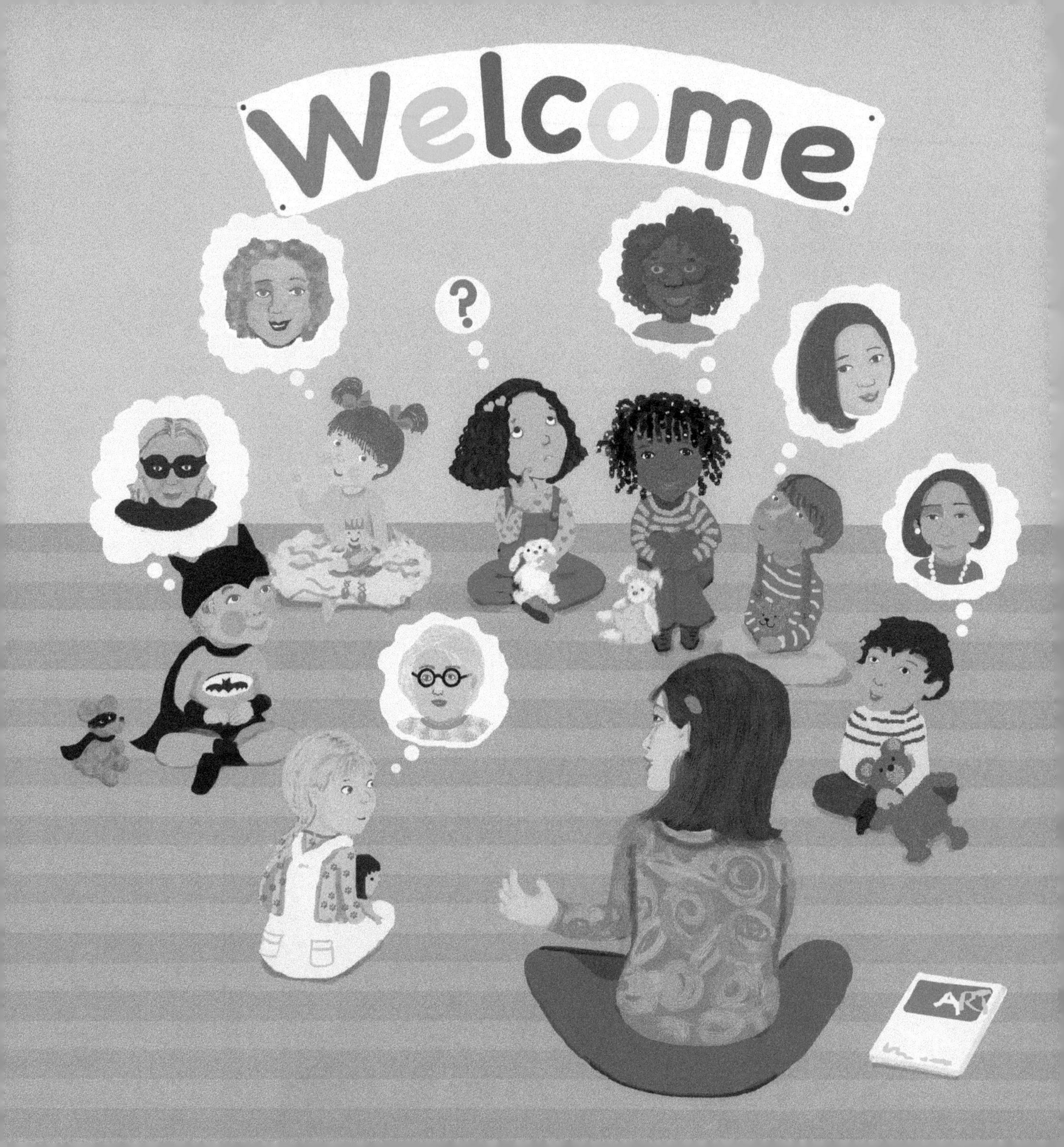
Welcome
?
ART

My
Nonna

During the day, my *nonna*, Giovanna, took care of me until I was old enough to go to kindergarten.

She only spoke to me in Italian, and I didn't know how to speak English (so I did not grow up speaking it).

On the first day of kindergarten, my *nonna* took me to school.

The teacher spoke in English, and sometimes I didn't understand her.

One day we were all in a circle. The teacher asked us, "What is your grandmother's name?"

"My grandmother's name is Teresa," said Evelyn.

"My grandmother's name is Lilly," said Ann, laughing.

Laura's grandmother was called Jane.

Everyone had a grandmother, except me!

When the teacher asked me what my grandmother's name was, I said, "I don't have a grandmother."

I was very upset.

When my *nonna* came to pick me up, I was very sad and she asked me, "What's wrong?"

"Nonna, I don't have a grandmother!" I told her sadly.

She was surprised and said, "*Ma che dici?* (What are you saying?) I am your grandmother." She gave me a big hug. "In Italian, *nonna* means grandmother."

I was so happy to hear this.

The next day, I went to school and told everyone, "I have a grandmother."

My friend Danny said his grandmother was born in Colombia, and he calls her *Abuela*.

Jolanta's grandmother lives in Poland, and she calls her *Babcia*.

Celine is French-Canadian, and she calls her grandmother *Grand-mère*.

George whispered to me, "I call my grandmother *Yiayia*," and we both laughed. His grandmother came from Greece.

Freda's grandmother visits her every year when she comes from Germany, and she calls her *Oma*.

Everyone was happy for me that I have a grandmother.

A Day with
My Nonna

I like spending a day with my nonna. We have fun. She is very smart.

When she first sees me, she opens her arms and says, "*Amore di Nonna.* (My love.)"

She then adds, "*Sbrigati a farti grande, così Nonna ti porta in bicicletta.* (Hurry up and grow up, so we can go bike riding.)"

"*Andremo a pattinare sul ghiaccio.* (We will ice skate together.)"

"*Ora andiamo al cinema e anche alla biblioteca.* (Now we will go to the movie theatre and to the library together.)"

Many of Nonna's books are in Italian. When she reads to me, I like the way it sounds.

After breakfast, sometimes we visit a friend named Teresa who speaks Italian too. She welcomes me with a big hug and kisses me too much.

"*Che bella bambina. Quanti anni hai?* (What a beautiful girl. How old are you?)" she says.

"Seven," I say.

"*Sette?*" she responds and always looks surprised.

"*Quanto sei alta!* (You are so tall!)" she says and shakes her head.

"*Ti piacciono i biscotti?* (Do you like cookies?)" Teresa asks while she pinches my cheek.

"*Sì, grazie* (Yes, thank you)," I say and take one.

"*Prendine un altro* (Take one more)," she insists.

Nonna has *espresso*, and I have *caffellatte*. *Espresso* is strong Italian coffee made with a special coffee maker. *Caffellatte* is mostly milk with very little coffee.

Nonna and Teresa laugh and talk about grown-up things.

"*Grazie per la visita* (Thank you for the visit)," Teresa says.

"*Torna a trovarmi presto* (Come and visit soon)," she yells while she's waving to us.

My nonna and I wave goodbye and say, "*Arrivederci*," and we leave.

We walk home chatting in both Italian and English. She always ends her conversation with "*Capito?* (Do you understand?)" My nonna wants to make sure that I do.

I repeat, "*Sì, Nonna, ho capito.* (Yes, Nonna, I understand.)"

She smiles and we walk hand in hand.

My Nonna
Is Italian

My nonna was born in Italy. She speaks to me in Italian.

"*Ciao, Franca, come stai?*" she asks me. I know it means, "Hi, Franca, how are you?"

"*Bene, Nonna, e tu?* (I am well, Nonna, and you?)" I answer her.

She nods with a smile, which means she is well. "*Bene.*"

We play a game called *Parliamo Italiano*, or Let's Speak Italian.

She teaches me how to say words like *buongiorno* (good morning).

Arrivederci is goodbye.

Il pranzo è pronto means lunch is ready.

I can count to ten: *uno*, *due*, *tre*, *quattro*, *cinque*, *sei*, *sette*, *otto*, *nove*, *e dieci*.

My nonna drives *l'automobile*, which is her car.

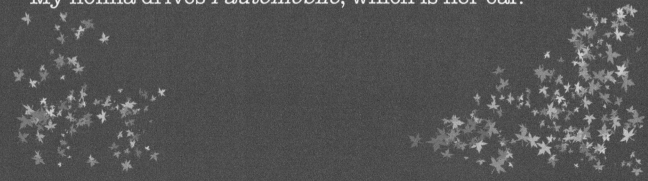

I remember words like *pane* (bread), *tavolo* (table), and *caramella* (candy).

When you least expect it, she will say, "*Dammi un bacio e un abbraccio.* (Give me a hug and a kiss.)"

So I give them to her.

She always asks, "*Hai fame?* (Are you hungry?)" but sometimes I am not.

"*No grazie, Nonna, non ho fame.* (No thank you, Nonna, I'm not hungry.)"

But she feeds me anyway. "*Se non mangi, non ti farai grande come me* (If you don't eat, you won't get big like me)," she says.

She always makes my favourite treat: bread with chocolate spread called Nutella.

"*La cioccolata sul pane é molto buona.* (Chocolate on bread is delicious.)" I agree with her.

Luglio
1 2 3 4 5 6
8 9 10 11
14 15 16
19 20 21
25 26 27

Insalata

FRANCA

NONNA

Lunch at
My Nonna's

My nonna is the best *cuoca* (cook) in the world. Pasta is always served at lunchtime, and it's served with bread and salad.

Her tomato sauce is made with real tomatoes. She has many jars of her homemade sauce in a cold storage called *la cantina*.

When lunch is almost ready, we set *la tavola* (the table).

"*Che cosa vuoi mangiare?* (What would you like to eat?)" asks Nonna.

"*Io voglio la pasta!* (I would like pasta!)" I answer.

I am excited when she asks me, "*Che tipo di pasta vuoi?* (What kind of pasta would you like?)"

I'll think about it while I set the table. This is not easy to answer.

Pasta is made with flour and water, and it comes in all sizes and shapes.

My *nonna* has all types of pasta: *spaghetti*, *rigatoni*, *penne*, *farfalline*, and *ruotine*. These are only a few.

Can you help me name some more?

The table is all set with piatti (plates).

I decide my favorite pasta is the butterfly wings called *farfalline*.

They taste so . . . yummy!

"*Io voglio mangiare le farfalline* (I want to eat the butterfly pasta)," I say.

"*Per secondo che vuoi?* (What would you like to eat after?)" she asks me.

"*Pane e mortadella!* (Bread with mortadella!)" I say excitedly.

Mortadella is a cold cut meat like ham. It is my favourite.

Nonna likes it when I eat.

I eat because I want to grow up to be just like her.

My Nonna's Family

My nonna came from Italy a long time ago on a big *nave* (ship) called *La Saturnia*. She came with her mother, father, brother, and sister.

She did not speak English. She went to school to learn how to read, write, and speak English.

Nonna's mother is very nice; she is my *bisnonna* (great-grandmother). We call her *Nonna-Grande* (Bigger Grandmother) because she is older.

She kisses and hugs me, gives me candies, and pinches my cheeks.

She knits me *maglie* (sweaters), and while she knits she tells me about her village in Italy.

She calls me *Bella* (Beautiful).

I have an uncle I call *Zio* and an aunt I call *Zia*.

My little *cugini* (cousins), Jessica and Julia, are younger than me.

Nonna-Grande tells us stories about the old village where she lived in Italy. They worked in the fields, and at the end of the season, they harvested wheat, fruit, and olives.

With the *farina di grano* (wheat), they made bread and pasta.

With *frutta* (fruit), they made *marmellata* (jam). With *uva* (grapes), they made *vino* (wine).

She was young when she left her village for Canada.

"Italy is far away," says my *nonno* (grandfather). He was born in Italy too. His town is called Ceprano. "To go to Italy, you must go by plane because it is very far."

"*Un giorno andremo in Italia* (One day we will go to Italy)," he tells me.

I know where Italy is on the map. It does not look that far away.

My *nonno* says, "Italy looks like a boot."

I agree with him.

Just take a look on the map.

My Nonna's Garden

In my *nonna's* garden, her flowers are all different colours.

Her vegetable garden has carrots and cucumbers.

In spring, the first flowers that bloom are yellow.

My *nonna's* favourite flowers are *la ginestra* and *la mimosa*.

She says, "*In Canada, la ginestra e la mimosa non crescono perché fa troppo freddo.* (In Canada, the ginestra and the mimosa don't grow. It's too cold.)"

In her garden she names all her flowers: *margherita* (daisy), *rosa* (rose), *geranio* (geranium) *lilly* (lily), and *tulipani* (tulips).

"*Le rose del mio giardino sono variopinte* (The roses in my garden are multicoloured)," she says, "*rosse, gialle, bianche, rosa, e arancioni* (red, yellow, white, pink, and orange)."

My nonna smiles and is happy to see her garden with butterflies and bees that settle on the flowers in her garden.

"*Le farfalle e le api sono insetti molto utili per impollinare* (The butterflies and the bees are insects that are very useful for pollination)," she explains.

I just say, "*Sì!* (Yes!)"

However, she does not like the squirrels going into the garden.

"*Lo scoiattolo mangia i pomodori* (Squirrels will eat the tomatoes)," she says.

My *nonna's* vegetable garden is not to be stepped on or she will say, "*Mannaggia la miseria!*" which is her favourite saying. I'm not sure exactly what it means, but it's something like "Good grief!"

Nonna grows tomatoes, *zucchine* (zucchini), *cipolle* (onions), and *fagiolini* (beans).

Il giardino di mia nonna è grande e meraviglioso. (My nonna's garden is big and wonderful.)

YOUR ORIGIN

* * * *

LE TUE ORIGINE

Where was your nonna born?
(*Dove è nata la tua nonna?*)

_____

Where was your nonno born?
(*Dove è nato il tuo nonno?*)

_____

In what regions of Italy were they born?
(*Quale regione sono nati?*)

Nonno: _____   Nonna: _____

Colour the regions where your grandparents were born.
(*Colora la regione dei tuoi Nonni.*)

CPSIA information can be obtained
at www.ICGtesting.com
Printed in the USA
BVHW021727220321
603180BV00009B/1241